T0064346

Do You Remember My Name?

When God Seems Distant

Stephanie M. Captain

authorHOUSE®

AuthorHouse™
1663 Liberty Drive
Bloomington, IN 47403
www.authorhouse.com
Phone: 1-800-839-8640

Published by AuthorHouse 4/18/2013

ISBN: 978-1-4817-4440-9 (sc)
ISBN: 978-1-4817-4441-6 (e)

Table of Contents

Dedication

To God the Father
Who saved me by His Son
And guides me through His Spirit

My hubby and best friend–Honey I love you more today than when I first said, "I Do" 27 years ago.

My children—
To my courageous and first born Amos and my daughter Chantal who has the spirit of Ruth.

To the beautiful, strong, faithful woman I am pleased to call daughter, Ashley.

My Aaron who makes me laugh and celebrate life.

And to my grandsons Simien and Asher who have stolen my heart—I love you.

My mother–Beulah
You light up my life

To my niece
Kimberlee-Michelle

And my friend and sister
Kesha Waldon
I can never forget you

Pastors "P" and "G" you push me, pray for me, and believe in me—I'm grateful.

Finally, to anyone that has ever been through anything, this book is for you.

Acknowledgements

To my sisters

My brothers

My friends

My family

My god-parents

My god-children

My Pastors

My church family

Thanks for loving me and supporting me

Chosen

It wasn't talent

Or He would have walked right by

It wasn't gifting, I had none

Except what He gave to me

I dare not say it was physical attraction

Because He does not consider that

He just decided and that was enough

Keep me as the apple of the eye, hide me under the shadow of thy wings, (Psalm 17:8).

PART 1

After the promise

All of us have been through or will go through a hardship or grueling period in life. Maybe even now you might be in a time or period where you feel forgotten. When you may have what seems like a thousand questions that there seem to be no solution. Things you just don't understand, can't figure out, or wonder why.

The process of this book has been over ten years. The five it took for me to get to the place where I thought it was finished and the five plus more years before God got me to the place to where I knew He had completed this work. Written as a result of having been at a point in my life when I believed the world was at my disposal, when I had so many promises from the Lord, then I suddenly found myself in the process.

By definition, a process means: proceeding, advance; **a natural phenomenon marked by a gradual change that leads to a particular result.**

Where you learn His purpose
Where you learn to kill the flesh and deal with emotions
Where you learn to fight for His presence

It is in the midst of the process that purpose and the presence of God is found. Whatever phenomenon had to be orchestrated to equal a process, God set up before you ever got to this earth. God did whatever necessary to bring you forth with mantle in hand and purpose in heart. Everyone's process is different, but the results are the same, purpose. If the flesh and emotions are not dealt with you will find yourself bitter not better. You may feel as if God has forgotten about you because you may find yourself along during this time. In the process you must remember your promise and realize that God can never lie.

Many Christians are in a continual process because of their character. The process will lead you to the path of purpose, but only character will keep you on that path. You will never be successful in your purpose until your character has been processed.

Know that a Promise always precedes the Process

"I had awakened so aware of His presence. I could sense Him in such a way it seemed my body was waking up from a night's rest, but my spirit had been communing with Him long before I opened my eyes. I felt total peace and I did not want to disturb it by moving one muscle. So I lay there in silence, waiting, listening as if to continue some unfinished conversation. Then, He spoke; a promise, four simply words that would change my life forever, 'I will prosper you.'

It had not just been solely the words that meant so much, but the gentleness in which He said them. They spoke volumes deep down to my soul. So deep, no matter what happened in my life from that moment on, I could not forget the promise.

Those four little words had not just come unexpectedly. They were an answer to my heart's cry. I remember sensing in my walk with God perhaps He wanted to use me in some way to bring Him glory and honor. I knew deep down that He was going to bless me with plenty, and that scared me. I knew I would without a doubt be blessed to be a blessing, but somehow this still made me a little nervous. I didn't know if I could handle it. I loved God and He was my desire, but I wanted nothing to come between us. Could I bear his anointing and His prosperity? All of this uncertainty prompted me to seek God in a way I never had.

There was an urgency in my pursuit that demanded His attention. I knew spiritual wealth would bring the balance to any other type of gain. Thus, for months I sought the Lord; not for money, but for Him. I longed for and craved God. I'd finally come to a point in life that I realized I was flesh and subject to weaknesses. I realized how dependent I was on God and knew that I could absolutely do nothing without Him. I found that even the desire to do so began to diminish. I wanted God, His ways, His statues, His integrity, His love and nothing could substitute for Him. So day after day I'd pray to Him. Waking up in the wee hours of the morning to talk to Him. I'd go back in the afternoon to talk to Him, then again in the evening I'd return. My concern was spiritual prosperity. Without this, what was the point? Finally, one morning He spoke. I knew exactly what He meant. "I will prosper you", inside and outside, I could rest. At least that is what I thought, not realizing war had just been waged because of those four little words, but it was NO surprise to God. He knew He had equipped me."

The enemy will come after the promise but he cannot have it unless you give it to him.

Learn from the scriptures

Joseph

The Word of God does not record details of what happens to Joseph between the time he was sold into slavery and the time he arrived in Egypt. It does not tell us what emotional trauma he suffered as a result of the betrayal of his own brothers. It doesn't record the grief in detail of the father who thought he would never see his son again. Yet I'm sure that somewhere along that journey Joseph made up his mind to hold on to his dream. He made a conscious decision to remember his dream and allow this to keep him going. He made a decision to trust the God of his fathers and to trust in the God he had been told so much about.

A considerable amount of time passed between Joseph's dream and its manifestation. Joseph was 17 when he was sold and 30 when that dream became a reality. The amazing thing is that whatever he encountered during this time frame was all a part of God's plan for his life. It was all connected to his purpose and the destiny of his family.

We do know that God:
Never left Joseph
Genesis 39:2
And the Lord was with Joseph, and he was a prosperous man; and he was in the house of his master the Egyptian.

We also know that Joseph:
Kept his integrity in tact
He obeyed and feared God
Remained in line with the plan of God despite adversity

The promise
Genesis 37:5-11 NKJ
Now Joseph had a dream, and he told it to his brothers; and they hated him even more. So he said to them, "Please hear this dream which I have dreamed:

There we were, binding sheaves in the field. Then behold, my sheaf arose and also stood upright; and indeed your sheaves stood all around and bowed down to my sheaf."

And his brothers said to him, "Shall you indeed reign over us? Or shall you indeed have dominion over us?" So they hated him even more for his dreams and for his words.

Then he dreamed still another dream and told it to his brothers, and said, "Look, I have dreamed another dream. And this time, the sun, the moon, and the eleven stars bowed down to me."

So he told it to his father and his brothers; and his father rebuked him and said to him, "What is this dream that you have dreamed? Shall your mother and I and your brothers indeed come to bow down to the earth before you?"

And his brothers envied him, but his father kept the matter in mind.

Dream fulfilled
Genesis 42:6-9
And Joseph was the governor over the land, and he it was that sold to all the people of the land: and Joseph's brethren came, and bowed down themselves before him with their faces to the earth.

And Joseph saw his brethren, and he knew them, but made himself strange unto them, and spake roughly unto them; and he said unto them, Whence come ye? And they said, From the land of Canaan to buy food.

And Joseph knew his brethren, but they knew not him.

And Joseph remembered the dreams which he dreamed of them, and said unto them, Ye are spies; to see the nakedness of the land ye are come.

The purpose of the journey
Genesis 45:4-9
And Joseph said unto his brethren, Come near to me, I pray you. And they came near. And he said, I am Joseph your brother, whom ye sold into Egypt.

Now therefore be not grieved, nor angry with yourselves, that ye sold me hither: for God did send me before you to preserve life.

For these two years hath the famine been in the land: and yet there are five years, in the which there shall neither be earing nor harvest.

And God sent me before you to preserve you a posterity in the earth, and to save your lives by a great deliverance.

So now it was not you that sent me hither, but God: and he hath made me a father to Pharaoh, and lord of all his house, and a ruler throughout all the land of Egypt.

Haste ye, and go up to my father, and say unto him, Thus saith thy son Joseph, God hath made me lord of all Egypt: come down unto me, tarry not:

Sometimes it helps to know what is in your bloodline

Joseph's Ancestry

To understand Joseph better you must take a look at his ancestry, his physical and spiritual blood line. Joseph himself was the result of a promise being fulfilled.

Genesis 30:22-24
And God remembered Rachel, and God hearkened to her, and opened her womb.

And she conceived, and bare a son; and said, God hath taken away my reproach:
And she called his name Joseph; and said, The LORD shall add to me another son.

Joseph was born out of a people that knew how to seek God and get results. They knew how to hold on to the Word of God until what he had promised came to fruition. Joseph's mother Rachel had been barren. His great-grandmother Sarah had been barren. All believed God and the end result was a son. Sometimes they tried to help God out a little, but this still did not stop their desire from coming to pass.

When we go through tough times we tend to think we're forgotten. It is an emotionally trying time, but we cannot be ruled by our emotions. Somehow we feel disconnected from God in the process. Feelings of loneliness, abandonment, and grief can bombard us. We may cry out to God do you remember me? What you have promised me. Are you not familiar with me anymore? Oh, Lord, remember me. The destiny that I have in the earth realm. How I fit jointly with the destinies of the body of Christ. Don't let that be aborted in me. Don't let me die unknown and unfulfilled. Remember me!

Samson cried this and God empowered him for his greatest victory. The thief cried these words before the death of Jesus Christ on the cross and passed from death to life, the ultimate paradise. Hannah cried, "Remember me" in barrenness and became fruitful. Joseph said these same words to the Baker while serving a prison sentence in Pothifer's dungeon.

Remember according to Webster's dictionary means to bring to mind or think of again, to keep in mind for attention for consideration, to retain in the memory.

Deal with the truth

Because God has said, "Never will I leave you; will I forsake you." Hebrews 13:5cNIV

For He [God] Himself has said, I will not in any way fail you nor give you up nor leave you without support. [I will] not in any degree leave you helpless nor forsake nor let [you] down (relax My hold on you)! [Assuredly not!] Hebrews 13c Amplified

And lo, I am with you always, even unto the end of the world. Amen Matthew 28:20b

And behold, I am with you all the days (perpetually, uniformly, and on every occasion), to the [very] close and consummation of the age. Amen (So be it). Matthew 38:20b Amplified

Vine's definition
Leave: "to send, to let go, loosen, forbear"

Forsake: "to leave behind, among, leave surviving," "to forsake, abandon, leave in straits, or helpless

According to Webster
Leave: to terminate association with: withdraw from, to go away, desert, abandon.

Forsake: to renounce or turn away from entirely

This is something God gave to me during my process:

I may not be able to feel Him
I may not see Him
I may not hear Him
But I know He's here
Because I have His Word
And they cannot be separated
I have His Word
He will come for it
I may feel He's abandoned me
His Word says He cannot and will not
I may feel forsaken
His Word says He will not
My circumstances may look like
He has left me behind in a strait
His Word says He would not
So all I have to do is wait

Wait for the next time I feel His touch
Wait for the next time I hear His voice
Wait for the next time I see Him

Unless He comes to take me home
There is always a next time
Wait is just in between now and the next time
His Word is what brings them together again

He cannot abandon His Word
He will not leave it unattended
He would not ignore its cry

Spirit calls to spirit
Word calls to word
Response is the voice
Voice is the answer

The answer
I felt you
I saw you
I'm with you

The next time

Sometimes you go through things so harsh it would appear that God has forgotten about you. It is during these times of turmoil that many promises and dreams have been aborted. Unless you carry your promise in your heart, times of tragedy, hardship, and trials can make it seem like they will never come to pass. They can make you doubt yourself and your ability to hear from God.

The Word says that the truth will make us free. Free from worry, anxiety, or anything that would try to keep you in bondage. The Bible also says in II Corinthians 13:8, you can do nothing against the truth, it will stand. You must fight with the truth and you will prevail. Whatever it is God has spoken to you about your purpose and destiny, hold on to it and guard it with your life. Jeremiah 29:11 can be a constant companion during the in between stages. **" For I know the thoughts *and* plans that I have for you, says the Lord, thoughts *and* plans for welfare *and* peace and not for evil, to give you hope in your final outcome."** (Amplified Bible) The final outcome is what God says and anything else that presents itself is just a test, a temptation, or a trick.

You must deal with feelings of abandonment. If not they can lead to:

Self-pity
Depression
Anger
Loneliness
Lethargy
Defiance
Disobedient

All of which will cause you to not want to communicate with your very source of deliverance.

You don't want to talk to God
You don't want to go to church
You don't want to read your Bible
You don't want to be around others
You're unhappy
You are restless
You are unfocused

This is a danger zone because what you don't want to do will turn into what you can't do because you allowed these feelings to linger too long. You become too familiar with them and now they have you captive. This happens too often to the saints of God. Remember God hemmed you in for His purpose.

Loneliness

This is an enemy you must dismiss, not fight, but oust from your presence. Engagement in battle with this is only a distraction from your real purpose; communion with God. This time is God's time. Set aside to build you in spirit, soul, and body. It is not a punishment, but a privilege.

Don't put yourself in solitary confinement

You will be tempted to shut down
You will be tempted to keep everybody and everything out

Remember:

In His (God's) captivity you can hear from God
In your captivity you cannot

In His (God's) captivity you can discern

In your own you cannot

You cannot allow disappointments to draw you into your own prison. There is neither release nor relief there; only you and them. Don't allow emotions to become a prison to you. Don't be afraid to bang on the bars that try to keep you closed in. Challenge them. You must challenge sickness, fear, death, pain, poverty, sin. They don't own you and they can't have you. Disobedience is something you must simply release yourself from to be free. This one is a choice. You either choose to obey or disobey.

One day God spoke this to my heart. "Depression is the fruit of fear." Fear that the thing I long for will not happen. Thus, an overwhelming sadness comes over you to try and compensate for great loss. I then realized, if I really trust God, I wouldn't be so down and out about what I say I am sure He will do.

The Struggle

Usually when God calls us to a higher level in Him we must go through some type of process or change. No different than our ancestors that we find by reading the Word of God. You may feel lead to get up earlier to pray, to fast more, to intercede more, or maybe to read or study more. It doesn't matter how long you're been saved or how spiritual you may be. To get certain results, it takes certain changes. This process is not to be confused with things that have to be endured because of disobedience or rebellion.

The struggle comes when it is time for a shift from mediocrity to extraordinary. You come to a place where time is up and you can no longer remain in the place of okay and effect the Kingdom. God allows you a certain amount of time to grow and then He places a mandate on you to impact the world around you greater than His Son did. It doesn't happen overnight. He allows you to become uncomfortable with mediocrity through the steps He has ordered for you.

The promise is: I will never leave you; I will personally escort you from battle to battle and from blessing to blessing. I will attend to you. I will comfort you. I will establish you. The resolve is: I know He's there, I know He loves me, anything else we can handle together.

The Process Challenges our Mindsets

In Matthew, it tells of the faith of a Canaanite woman. These passages of scriptures have never really been my favorite to be quite honest. There was just something about them that seem to offend me just a little bit, until I grabbed hold of the mentally of the woman, the desperation of the woman, and the humility of the woman.

Matthew 15:21-28
Then Jesus went thence, and departed into the coasts of Tyre and Sidon.

And, behold, a woman of Canaan came out of the same coasts, and cried unto him, saying, Have mercy on me, O Lord, thou Son of David; my daughter is grievously vexed with a devil.

But he answered her not a word. And his disciples came and besought him, saying, Send her away; for she crieth after us.

But he answered and said, I am not sent but unto the lost sheep of the house of Israel.

Then came she and worshipped him, saying, Lord, help me.

But he answered and said, It is not meet to take the children's bread, and to cast to the dogs.

And she said, Truth, Lord: yet the dogs eat of the crumbs which fall from their masters' table.

Then Jesus answered and said unto her, O woman, great is thy faith: be it unto thee even as thou wilt. And her daughter was made whole from that very hour.

Upon a first glimpse it appeared she asked for help and Jesus:

1. Ignored her

2. The disciples shunned her

3. Jesus referred to her as a dog (the heathen nation that she represented)

I felt I needed something from God, just as she did so this text was somehow connected to me, but I grasped the wrong portion. My focus initially was on the response of Jesus when it should have been on the woman. Her mentality was one of tenacity and humility.

The very first thing she did was:

1. Worship Him

    Jesus' answer to this is noted in verse 26.

    But he answered and said, it is not meet to take the children's bread, and to cast it to dogs.

    Now personally, by now my feelings would have been hurt and I would have gone home believing I would have to live with a possessed child for the rest of my life.

2. This is her response: she agrees with Jesus

    She acknowledges who she is and what she came from

    27And she said truth, Lord, yet the dogs eat the crumbs which fall from the master's table.

3. She humbled herself

> Her state of mind was this; although I'm in the position I'm in, I'm still tasting of your goodness. I've sampled enough to know I want more, I need more. You're the only one that can help me. Without you my seed will die in the state it's in.

Jesus was not directly referring to her, but to a heathen Nation, but she refused to be classified with everyone else despite what she was born into. Humble yourself, admit it's you and don't make excuses for past failures or mistakes. Be radical in your decision to walk out your purpose and toss out every care about everything except His will, His purpose, and His divine destiny for your life. Let me warn you, when you realize what your destiny is hell will fight you to keep you tied to the past, genealogy, your weakness, and anything else that will keep you from advancing the Kingdom of God with your prophetic destiny.

Hence the battle begins.

The Real Fight

Satan's number one tactic is mind games, i.e. thought patterns and strongholds. If he can gain a foothold in your thought patterns, it is only a matter of time before you act out under his influence. Even though God has given us the helmet of salvation, because this is the battleground that determines victory or defeat, many Christians are still losing because they have not gained control over what they meditate on. We meditate on the wrong things. We see the bad in people rather than the good. We see the glass as half empty rather than half full. We place our faith in what we see rather than what we don't see. We ponder what we don't understand, what we can't do, what we can't handle and build up strongholds in the mind only to be acted out at a later time. The Word of God, faith in God and meditation are a remedy for this.

Most Christian are familiar with Joshua 1:8 and Psalms 1:2

Joshua 1:8
Do not let this book of the Law depart from your mouth; mediate on it day and night, so that you may be careful to do everything written in it. Then you will be prosperous and successful.

Psalms 1:2
But his delight is in the law of the Lord, and of the Lord, and on his law he meditates day and night.

Meditation is so important because as I have stated, all our battles are begun here and it is also determined here whether we win or lose.

"It's all in the mind." We've all heard it or maybe even said it ourselves at one time or another. There is a negative and a positive to this saying.

Most people don't care to deal with people they believe are unstable in the mind. As an example, let's look at the hypochondriac. A hypochondriac believes something even though there is no physical evidence. It is embedded in the mind. Symptoms become a part of them because they have meditated on them. They convince themselves in the mind and when this happens it is transferred to the heart and the body acts out the symptoms. They have built up a stronghold. A defense around the mind that this is so (the illness), and thereby enclosed that thought pattern in, thus, they begin living it out. The pain is real, the symptoms are real. They have fortified their illness in their mind and their body will carry out those symptoms. This lets us know how powerful the mind is. If my mind is so important, then I need to spend a certain amounts of time meditating each day. Wouldn't you think?

One of my favorite scriptures comes from Philippians 4:7, and it says, and the peace of God which surpasses all understanding will guard your hearts and minds through Christ Jesus. When things get hectic I always refer back to this scripture. I keep this scripture as a part of my everyday life. When I dress myself or reinforce my armor (Eph. 6:10-18)

I meditate on this scripture. I close my eyes and say Father, I thank you that I have on the helmet of salvation. I thank you that the peace of God which passes all understanding guards my heart and my mind. Then I continue dressing in the armor while giving Him back His word.

This is what the Vine's dictionary says:

Guard-it comes from the Greek word phroureo. It is a military term that means to keep by guarding or to keep under guard, to block every way of escape, as in a siege.

But it doesn't stop there. This word not only refers to outward protection but it denotes the meaning of inward protection. The Holy Spirit keeps benevolent custody and watchful guardianship in view of worldwide idolatry.

When I was about thirteen I went to Washington D.C. for the first time. From this trip one experience is tattooed in my memory forever. I went to the tomb of the unknown soldier (at that time he remained unidentified). There posted at the grave site was a soldier and his only duty was to guard these tombs. He marched up and down, fully armed, ready to do battle with anyone that would attempt to harm that grave site in any way. He was protecting a precious monument from all intruders. What was really even more intriguing to me was the changing of the guard. When that particular soldier's duty was expired, there was an official change of guard so someone fresh and alert could take this job.

This is what meditation does: it sets up a defense.

The military also uses soldiers to perform what is referred to as "guard duty." The soldier is on duty for 24 hours to protect important places of operation or equipment, to fortify the military installation. Notice the time period; 24 hours, an entire day. I need to read, pray, and meditate daily. In the spiritual, we guard our heart and mind to fortify our spirit, soul and body. If not, rest assured anything that stays in the mind too long will move to the heart; sometimes undetected.

Proper meditation brings to life those things that are real or of eternal substance and silences those things that are not.

Conscious and sub-conscious meditation

This is what the Word of God tells us:
And He said to them, Be careful what ye are hearing. The measure [of thought and study] you give [to the truth you hear] will be the measure [of virtue and knowledge] that comes back to you—and more [besides] will be given to you who hear.
Mark 4:24 Amplified

Conscious meditation is self-initiated to build one's self up. It is a time to meditate on the written and spoken Word of God.
Sub-Conscious meditation allows those subconscious things to affect the thought pattern in a negative or positive way.

Have you ever been riding in an elevator and before you knew it you were singing or humming to the tune of the music? Many children become the victims of the negatives of wrong type of pleasure, and this makes them vulnerable to devices they know not of until it's too late many times. Certain kinds of music are an example of this. Because their minds are passive, they pick up on subliminal messages that can lead to spiritual and sometimes physical death eventually if allowed to progress. The suicide rate is alarming in our society.

When you learn to use this realm as a positive it becomes powerful. I HEAR it, but it has NO affect on me as far as the negative goes. We should be in the world but not of the world.

Over the years I have come to hold a few personal rules about meditation near and dear. I must sleep, but my spirit never does. So when I am challenged; be it in body, personal life or in my thinking, I use mediation as an added dose of medication to my situation. I find everything I can on the subject and add it to what I have already been taught and I regurgitate it until I see results. During these times there are some things I do not allow to become habit in my life.

1. **I never sleep with the television playing over me (unless I have purposely set a Christian station).**

   I may have fallen asleep with something godly on, but nine times out of ten when I awake during the night it would be killing or some other content that causes your spirit to be restless. Thus, the nightmares and tiredness that may be experienced as a result because I've fed myself with negativity all night long. This is the atmosphere I allowed myself to rest in and become unguarded in so to speak. This works great for troubled children.

   Psalms 63:6 CEV
   I think about you before I go to sleep, and my thoughts turn to you during the night.

   Psalms 119:148 Amplified
   My eyes anticipate the night watches and I am awake before the cry of the watchmen that I may meditate on your word.

   If something is too big for me, I use this method and it works every time. You will roll over at night and hear your spirit rehearsing the scriptures you've fed yourself.

2. **When I know I'm going into a battle zone, I prepare**

   If I know I'm going to be put in a situation where everything I stand for is going to be challenged for a period a time, I set up defenses.

As Christians we are called to compel men to come to Christ. It may just be me or you God calls to that place Christians are forbidden to go to bring someone out, just know it is God that told you to go. He may place you in a place of darkness for a period of time just to be a light. If you are not settled in the mind and heart the enemy will try to intimidate in these areas. One of the saddest things I've witnessed in the church is seeing a Christian get in a realm they are unprepared or seasoned and the enemy pulls them back into the same mess they were trying to deliver someone else from.

Meditation is more than a feeling, it is a fortress. Now let me just say this; meditation is not being or even looking like you are in la la land. Many times in your day to day activities you can implement meditation and the only evidence anyone has is the peace they benefit from while in your presence.

Note:
It is imperative for every Christian to do certain preparation during certain seasons, whether things are going good and if times are challenging. Just as the Jews according to the Bible have certain customs and seasons that are observed throughout the year, so should we. I do not recommend that any person enter anything new, i.e. new job, relationship, home, church, new year, etc. without taking time to hear from God and get clear instructions and directions. Find out what He says about the situation and get His wisdom for your new arena. This alone will cut down on a lot of what we call Crisis in our lives.

3. **I only meditate on the scriptures and the spoken Word of God**

There will be times in your life when you must do just like Jesus did.

Luke 5:35-40:

While He was still speaking, there came some from the ruler's house, who said [to Jairus], Your daughter has died. Why bother *and* distress the Teacher any further?

Overhearing but ignoring what they said, Jesus said to the ruler of the synagogue, Do not be seized with alarm *and* struck with fear; only keep on believing.

And He permitted no one to accompany Him except Peter and James and John the brother of James.

When they arrived at the house of the ruler of the synagogue, He looked [carefully and with understanding] at [the] tumult and *the people* weeping and wailing loudly.

And when He had gone in, He said to them, Why do you make an uproar and weep? The little girl is not dead but is sleeping.

And they laughed *and* jeered at Him. But He put them all out, and, taking the child's father and mother and those who were with Him, He went in where the little girl was *lying.*),

Follow Jesus's example. You have to kick everybody out. In this case, all negativity and nay sayers. It is the only way you can change your mind set. Think on what Jesus said, Jesus did, How He said it, How He did it, The promises of God and what they mean to you and your situation. Think on these things until you dream them, see them when you are wide awake, speak them despite circumstance; believe them without a shadow of a doubt. Keep God's Word ever before you. Play it while you sleep. Listen to it while you are riding in the car. Talk about it with your friends that believe like you believe. Declare it out loud when you have your alone time with God. Put it on note cards and keep it with you so that when you get a moment you can rehearse it. Put it on sticky notes on the refrigerator, bathroom mirror, but keep it close and until there is no space between you and it.

Walking out your Destiny

Walking out my destiny at times can seem quite overwhelming. Exciting, yet overwhelming at the same time. To me it's like walking the Atlanta Ocean. I'm enjoying the scenic beauty, the peace of the water, the smell of the ocean and suddenly I realize I don't know how to swim. Suddenly, I remember I didn't get there by my own power. I've come face to face with the reality of my own inability. Without warning I feel the need to understand the natural laws of my surrounding, thus causing me to become overwhelmed and I begin to sink. I'd been so busy walking and talking to him I never noticed us leaving the shore. I never perceived the sand under my feet give way to water. I was so enclosed in our conversation, our time together, the way He listened, the He spoke, all else had before inferior. And now here I stood, water quickly rising to my waist; in a panic.

This is what it is like some days. You question yourself. How did I get here? Who told me I could do this? I can't swim! What could I have been thinking to make such a step? Then you remember. It was those closet moments. Those closet promises. The *I will* and the *I shall*, He promised. The *you can* and the *you possess* He told you. Most of all it had been the, *my beloved* and the *you're mine* that had captivated me and drawn me directly into the deep. Which is exactly what and where it is; the deep. The place of no return. The place where you say, God if I die trusting you, I just die, but I won't turn around. Wherever you lead me, that is where I will go. We're in this together for the long haul, it's me and you.

PART 2

Where is God?

When my children were smaller there was a popular show on television called, *Where in the world is Carmen Sandiego?* The show's main purpose was to track down or find the infamous Carmen so that justice could be served. It was the job of the contestants to locate her based on clues given to them from their leader. She could be anywhere in the world and what you learned about her, how she carried out certain tasks, and what she wore where all clues that aided in capturing her. It was then left up to you to figure it out. With God you never have to do this as a Christian.

It doesn't matter how long you have been a Christian or a Jesus follower, at some point and time in your journey you will if you have not already, wonder where God is. Where is God in my situation? How does He fit in the chaos of my now? Where is God when it comes to my next move? Where is God because perhaps if He knew about this it would never have happened or taken place. Where is God because I don't feel Him.

When my niece was murdered it was the most horrific thing I have ever been through. Oddly enough during that time I never questioned where God was in the situation. No, I did not understand why it happened. Yes, the pain was so great, but I never questioned where God was. I knew without a shadow of a doubt that the God I served was right there with me and my family. Why? Because I never would have made it otherwise. It was His strength and only His strength that allowed me to be by my brother's side, help make funeral arrangements, and say good-bye to her when she was in the prime of her life. No one else could do that for me. No one else could strengthen me and my family but God.

There will be times that you know, but then the other times will come. When you just want to know for sure. Just need a little extra assurance. When you need to feel His touch before you go, do, or say; even as you are getting through something.

All of us must grow up and mature at some time. Babies do not always drink milk, they graduate to meat. As they grow through phases, their diets change based on their needs. The bottle must be taken, the binkie must be thrown out, and they must at some point learn to feed themselves. They first learn to roll over, then slide, crawl, and eventually walk and run. They must learn how to be comfortable with others in safe environments and this process may cause them to go through separation anxiety. They just do not feel safe. They want their parent or caregiver, but the parent and caregiver knows they are safe. Despite the crying, which is hard to hear, the parents understands that their beloved infant, toddler, preschooler is in good hands. They understand that unless the child transitions it can be detrimental to them later in life. So it is with us spiritually.

The more you learn about God, His character, His Word, the less you will deal with having to prove He is who He says He is or He does what He promised He will do.

Babies deal with what they feel
Adults deal with what they know

Babies deal with what they see or do not see i.e. Mommy's not here, she won't ever return

Adults deal with what they have seen i.e. She has always returned so I will just wait until

This relationship with parent and child is built over a time period where trust has been established. Time that has proven that words always follow up with a corresponding action. Time that has lain a pattern of positive behavior, loving discipline, and unconditional love. So it is with the Christian and our heavenly Father.

Even as an adult or a more mature Christian you must develop your relationship with Christ or your actions will always retort back to that of an infant or a child. For example, you may know that God is everywhere as an adult, but as a more mature adult you know He is not just floating around in the atmosphere, but in you. Seeing to the affairs of your life. Working on your behalf and concerned about every intricate detail of your life.

The first step in following God is realizing you must never depend on your feelings, they can be most deceptive. Truth is your ally in every situation when it comes to the God of all gods. That truth is only found in His Word. Jesus said in John 14:6, "I am the way the truth and the life." Truth is the only thing that will or can free us when life attempts to wrestle us down with its cares.

It will not work well for an employer that calls in each week because they do not feel like going in to do the job they have promised to do. What if you did not feel like paying your mortgage for a period of time? Or getting up to feed your children. Perhaps, you do not feel like paying the electric bill. Would there be consequences? Of course.

All of those things seem a bit childish and even a bit naïve and so the average person knows enough not to adhere to those feelings because the consequences would be too great. What about in faith then?

F.E.E.L.

When you are standing on a promise, waiting for a change, believing God for a blessing you do not have the privilege to feel as it relates to whims. Feel in this sense means to:

Forget Every Evil Lie

If it is contrary to God's Word renounce it and denounce. It is not what you see but what He says. Always agree with God even if the world around you doesn't. Is this easy? No. But is it worth it? Yes. Sometimes you may have to say I am bold while shaking in your boots. Say I am strong while feeling weak in your body. Learn to bring your situations up to the truth. God's truth. How? By speaking it and coming into agreement with what He has said about you.

This does not mean that you do not feel pain, and trouble does not affect or effect your life. Your senses are alive and well. It means that you know it cannot last forever. It means that whatever you feel God does also, He is going through whatever you are going through right along with you.

I have had many midnight court sessions and hearings where I have had to take my accusers before the high court of God.

My symptoms
My feelings
Circumstances
Accusations
Friend betrayals
To get legal eviction notices. To enforce trespassing laws. To stand on my legal ground which is God's sovereign promises and Almighty power. I have stood before the highest court and pleaded my case. My legal ground in God's court taking numerous witnesses to testify with me and for me.

For healing
For deliverance
For mercy
For needs
For peace

Reliable Witnesses that only know truth to speak.
The Bible says in 2 Corinthians 13:8, "You can do nothing against the truth."

Witnesses that have done this before and know the system. The Word of The Lord has been tried.
Psalm 18:30

As for God, his way is perfect: the word of the LORD is proven: he is a shield to all those that trust in him.

Witnesses that never change their position
Isaiah 55:11 New Living Translation
It is the same with my word. I send it out, and it always produces fruit. It will accomplish all I want it to, and it will prosper everywhere I send it.

Hebrews 13:8 Amplified
Jesus Christ (the Messiah) is [always] the same, yesterday, today, [yes] and forever (to the ages).

John 3:16-18 Message
"This is how much God loved the world: He gave his Son, his one and only Son. And this is why: so that no one need be destroyed; by believing in him, anyone can have a whole and lasting life. God didn't go to all the trouble of sending his Son merely to point an accusing finger, telling the world how bad it was. He came to help, to put the world right again. Anyone who trusts in him is acquitted; anyone who refuses to trust him has long since been under the death sentence without knowing it. And why? Because of that person's failure to believe in the one-of-a-kind Son of God when introduced to him.

So where is God then? When things spin out of control. When life is so hard to bear. When you cannot see Him in your situation. Where is God? Right there inside of you.

Where is God?
Acts 17:27
That they should seek the Lord, if perhaps they might feel after him, and find him, though he be not far from every one of us:

Where is God?
Luke 17:21 Ampified
Nor will people say, Look! Here [it is]! or, See, [it is] there! For behold,

the kingdom of God is within you [in your hearts] *and* among you [surrounding you].

Where is God?
Colossians 1:27
To whom God was pleased to make known how great for the Gentiles are the riches of the glory of this mystery, which is Christ within *and* among you, the Hope of [realizing the] glory.

The truth is, God the Creator of the universe, Jesus the Messiah, brought all He is with Him when He was invited to live inside of you. All of His gifts. All of His power. All of His strength. Now you must draw from Him.

Draw from
Christ the healer
Isaiah 53:4-5
Surely he hath borne our griefs, and carried our sorrows: yet we did esteem him stricken, smitten of God, and afflicted. But he was wounded for our transgressions, he was bruised for our iniquities: the chastisement of our peace was upon him; and with his stripes we are healed.

Draw from
Christ the Prince of Peace
Isaiah 9:6
For a child is born to us, a son is given to us. The government will rest on his shoulders. And he will be called: Wonderful Counselor, Mighty God, Everlasting Father, Prince of Peace.

John 14:27
Peace I leave with you, my peace I give unto you: not as the world giveth, give I unto you. Let not your heart be troubled, neither let it be afraid.

Philippians 4:7 Amplified
And God's peace [shall be yours, that tranquil state of a soul assured

of its salvation through Christ, and so fearing nothing from God and being content with its earthly lot of whatever sort that is, that peace] which transcends all understanding shall garrison *and* mount guard over your hearts and minds in Christ Jesus.

Draw from
Christ the Redeemer
Galatians 3:13 Amplified
Christ purchased our freedom [redeeming us] from the curse (doom) of the Law [and its condemnation] by [Himself] becoming a curse for us, for it is written [in the Scriptures], Cursed is everyone who hangs on a tree (is crucified);

Galatians 3:23-26
But before faith came, we were kept under the law, shut up unto the faith which should afterwards be revealed.

Wherefore the law was our schoolmaster to bring us unto Christ, that we might be justified by faith.

But after that faith is come, we are no longer under a schoolmaster.

For ye are all the children of God by faith in Christ Jesus.

To communicate effectively with anyone you must know their language. What's His language…faith and love. They will take you farther, make you hold on longer, and keep you stronger in your walk.

Matthew 22:37 Amplified
And He replied to him, You shall love the Lord your God with all your heart and with all your soul and with all your mind (intellect).

Galatians 5:6
For in Jesus Christ neither circumcision avails anything, nor uncircumcision; but faith which works by love.

Hebrews 11:6

But without faith it is impossible to please him: for he that comes to God must believe that he is, and that he is a rewarder of them that diligently seek him.

Allow the Word to become an intimate part of your life and develop your relationship with God every chance you are given.

Colossian 3:16 New Living Translation

Let the message about Christ, in all its richness, fill your lives. Teach and counsel each other with all the wisdom he gives. Sing psalms and hymns and spiritual songs to God with thankful hearts.

Learn everything there is to know about the true and living God until you know His character, His ways, His heart; and then you will know just where He is.

If there is still question, or feeling of abandonment then you must ask yourself, is there a reason? If you feel far away from God, is there a reason?

Have I been disobedient? Am I too busy? Am I listening? Am I in the right position or place? Have I allowed something to come between us?

If you can answer yes to any of these questions then the remedy is simple. Return to God because He will never leave you. Repent and cultivate your relationship again. With God there is never a question as to if He cares or if He is there.

2 Corinthians 13:5-9 Message

"Test yourselves to make sure you are solid in the faith. Don't drift along taking everything for granted. Give yourselves regular checkups. You need firsthand evidence, not mere hearsay, that Jesus Christ is in you. Test it out. If you fail the test, do something about it. I hope the test won't show that we have failed. But if it comes to that, we'd rather the test showed our failure than yours. We're rooting for the truth to win out in you. We couldn't possibly do otherwise. We don't just put up with our limitations; we celebrate them, and then go on to celebrate every strength, every triumph of the truth in you. We pray hard that it will all come together in your lives."

PART 3

What's in a Name?

Your name identifies who you are.

What you are called and what you call your situation in many cases depends on your current status in many circumstances. This is unfortunate.

Know who you are---often times people will not tell you or if they do it will be according to what they see not what God predestined.

It is often very interesting what nick names families choose to call their children, spouses and friends. Pet names only people that share intimacy with them could know or be privy to. Names sometimes chosen based on an action done or witnessed in a past long before. Maybe even chosen because of something some other family member did or witnessed. Someone's hopes or dreams may birth other pet names. Some beloved relative or dear friend could bare the honor or dishonor of what we choose to respond to. What we are called and how we answer from the time we come into this world bares great significant.

Often what we are called is detrimental to our course in life. I found it very intriguing when I learned that Martin Luther King Jr. was called Michael the first five or six years of his life. Even more interesting was the fact that he was called "Mike" until about age twenty-two by family and friends. It was only after the late Dr. Martin Luther King's father traveled to Germany in 1934 and was so inspired by the German Protestant Martin Luther that upon returning to the United States his father changed his name to Martin and then his son's name was changed from Michael King to Martin Luther King in honor of this great man.

At five years old such a drastic change to what he had already answered to for so long; in school, by his friends, family, at church, and in his community. Yet God knew that he too would become a great Civil Rights leader in his own country and known to people all over the world for what he did to help a struggling people and a nation.

Michael to Martin

Michael means Who is like the Lord,

Martin means servant of mars, God of war
Lurther means people army

What's in a name...a future, a dream, an inheritance, and even a destiny.

In the book of Genesis we see where God himself makes the change for Abram to Abraham.

Abram to Abraham
The Process

Birth
Genesis 11:27
Now these are the generations of Terah: Terah begat Abram, Nahor, and Haran; and Haran begat Lot.

Promise
Genesis 12:1-5
Now the LORD had said unto Abram, Get thee out of thy country, and from thy kindred, and from thy father's house, unto a land that I will shew thee:

² And I will make of thee a great nation, and I will bless thee, and make thy name great; and thou shalt be a blessing:

³ And I will bless them that bless thee, and curse him that curseth thee: and in thee shall all families of the earth be blessed.

⁴ So Abram departed, as the LORD had spoken unto him; and Lot went with him: and Abram was seventy and five years old when he departed out of Haran.

⁵ And Abram took Sarai his wife, and Lot his brother's son, and all their substance that they had gathered, and the souls that they had gotten in Haran; and they went forth to go into the land of Canaan; and into the land of Canaan they came.

The Separation
Genesis 13:14-18

¹⁴ And the LORD said unto Abram, after that Lot was separated from him, Lift up now thine eyes, and look from the place where thou art northward, and southward, and eastward, and westward:

¹⁵ For all the land which thou seest, to thee will I give it, and to thy seed for ever.

¹⁶ And I will make thy seed as the dust of the earth: so that if a man can number the dust of the earth, then shall thy seed also be numbered.

¹⁷ Arise, walk through the land in the length of it and in the breadth of it; for I will give it unto thee.

¹⁸ Then Abram removed his tent, and came and dwelt in the plain of Mamre, which is in Hebron, and built there an altar unto the LORD.

Name change
Genesis 17:5

Neither shall thy name any more be called Abram, but thy name shall be Abraham; for a father of many nations have I made thee .

Note God told Abraham about his name being changed. Abraham was responsible for telling everyone else that who he was had changed. But he had to be the first to embrace it for himself; the fact that he was no longer Abram but Abraham.

Promise fulfilled
Genesis 21:3 KJV

And Abraham called the name of his son that was born unto him, whom Sarah bare to him, Isaac.

Abraham's promise is still being fulfilled on a daily basis as people of all nations and tongues are born into the faith and become members of the family of God through Christ Jesus.

Abram-exalted father

Abraham-father of a multitude, father of many nations

God always has a better plan. He went from being destined to be exalted within his household and family to being the father of faith to the entire family of Christ. According to his original name, Abraham was always intended to be a father, but after the name change he was a father to many nations.

Sarai to Sarah

Genesis 17:15
And God said unto Abraham, As for Sarai thy wife, thou shalt not call her name Sarai, but Sarah shall her name be.

In preparation for Sarai to enter into her purpose God had to change her name so that she could be prepared to receive the promise. In this case, Isaac and the world. All a part of the redemptive plan, Sarai and Abram stepped up to the plate and took over where Adam and Eve had left us and became the new spiritual parents of those that would be born again by grace through faith.

Sarai means dominative or a head person

Sarah means Lady, princess, or queen

Most people remember Sarah for being the wife of Abraham. Or that she laughed when God said she would have a baby. They seem to forget that Abraham laughed too (Genesis 17:17). Only there is much more to this woman of God whom the Bible and God himself says that she is our Mother. During Sarah's time it was considered a curse when you could not bear children. Children were the most valuable thing in life next to having a husband. After Sarah became an old woman I am sure all hopes of ever enjoying carrying a baby and giving birth were gone, until one day she overheard a conversation.

God's promise to Sarah
And I will bless her and give you a son also by her. Yes, I will bless her, and she shall be a mother of nations; kings of peoples shall come from her. (Genesis 17:16 Amplified)

It is important to notice the conflict that was in Sarah and Abraham's lives at the time they received the promise from God. God was on the brink of destroying Sodom; the place where Abraham's nephew lived. This was no small thing since Lot had traveled with Abraham when God told him to get from among his kindred. Abraham was the head of his family because his father had already died. Lot had been with his grandfather because his father passed on early and so Abraham took him under his wing. So the couple was faced with the joys of a promised child and the potential destruction of another relative.

God changed Abraham and Sarah keeping His promise in the midst of much trials and He will do the same thing for you.

A lesson to learn
You cannot call it like you see it….You have to call it by its purpose. At first it would appear that this practice first began with the Father of many nations Abraham but the truth is it started in the very beginning with God's creations.

Genesis 1:1-4
In the beginning God created the heavens and the earth.

The earth was without form, and void; and darkness *was* on the face of the deep. And the Spirit of God was hovering over the face of the waters. Then God said, "Let there be light"; and there was light.

And God saw the light, that *it was* good; and God divided the light from the darkness.

Three things here

1. Without form
2. Void
3. Darkness covered the face of the deep

God changed their name by calling them into their purpose

First:
He dealt with the darkness first

"He said, Let there be light"

You must have vision. You must be able to see in spite of and despite of. You need a vision to fuel your faith to keep going forward. Without a vision you will have no direction.

Scripture:
Without a vision the people stumble all over themselves. (Proverbs 29:18)

Next:
He dealt with the "without form"
"Called heaven"
"Called earth"

Then:
He dealt with the void
"Vegetation"
He made it to produce

What God said, He saw----we are made in His image and can be no different.

Did Abraham and Sarah live up to their names or destiny?

You will find them both in the hall of faith

Hebrews 11:8
By faith Abraham, when he was called to go out into a place which he should later receive for an inheritance, obeyed; and he went out, not knowing where he went.

Hebrews 11:17
By faith Abraham, when he was tested, offered up Isaac: and he that had received the promises offered up his only begotten son.

Hebrews 11:11-12
By faith Sarah herself also received strength to conceive seed, and she bore a child when she was past the age, because she judged Him faithful who had promised.

Therefore sprang there even of one, and him as good as dead, so many as the stars of the sky in multitude, and as the sand which is by the sea shore innumerable.

1 Peter 3:6
as Sarah obeyed Abraham, calling him lord, whose daughters you are if you do good and are not afraid with any terror.

Luke 1:73
The oath which He swore to our father Abraham:

Luke 13:16
So ought not this woman, being a daughter of Abraham, whom Satan has bound—think of it—for eighteen years, be loosed from this bond on the Sabbath?"

You will also find them in Romans and Colossians

Benoni changed to Benjamin

Benjamin was the great grandson of Abraham; his parents being Jacob and Rachel.

Genesis 35:16-18

[16] And they journeyed from Bethel; and there was but a little way to come to Ephrath: and Rachel travailed, and she had hard labour.

[17] And it came to pass, when she was in hard labour, that the midwife said unto her, Fear not; thou shalt have this son also.

[18] And it came to pass, as her soul was in departing, (for she died) that she called his name Benoni: but his father called him Benjamin.

Benoni in Hebrew (1126) son of my sorrows

Benjamin in Hebrew (1144) means son of my right hand (what does right hand signify…strength and power, place of honor)

Rachel called him what he gave her
Jacob called him what God gave him

You have to be real careful here because there is a common phrase that says, "I call it as I see it," but if you ever expect to get where God promised, you had better call it as He sees it, as He says it, and as He promised. Our eyes can deceive us and behaviors can mislead us, but truth is not moved by either one of these.

Genesis 35:18

And it came to pass, as her soul was in departing, (for she died) that she called his name Benoni: but his father called him Benjamin.

The difference in the names:

Benoni means:
Son of my sorrow or vanity

Benjamin means
Son of right hand, (represents strength and authority)

Important to note here:

- The mother said one thing
- The father said another
- The agreement had to come from God

Lesson

Sometimes people will speak to you based on where they are---She, Rachel was in pain so she wanted it to be known. Pain had been her condition; it should not have been placed on her child. Unfortunately, this is the case of many today; because of their turmoil, many are made to suffer. If you allow it of course; thank God Jacob did not. Thank God Jacob saw past the moment, the situation; he dared to see a future for his child. See a future for your child, grandchild, god-child, and Sunday school class, even when they cannot or it looks bleak. Call them what God calls them. These scriptures are helpful during times of challenge.

Joshua 24:15c
but as for me and my house, we will serve the LORD.

(My pastor, Pastor Pamela Gardner taught me to use this as a weapon).

Proverbs 11:21
Though hand join in hand, the wicked shall not be unpunished : but the seed of the righteous shall be delivered .

Did Benjamin live up to his name?

According to the Bible he had 10 sons

Genesis 43:34
And he took and sent messes unto them from before him: but Benjamin's mess was five times so much as any of their's. And they drank, and were merry with him.

Genesis 45:14
And he fell upon his brother Benjamin's neck, and wept; and Benjamin wept upon his neck.

Genesis 45:22
To all of them he gave each man changes of raiment; but to Benjamin he gave three hundred pieces of silver, and five changes of raiment.

Genesis 46:21
And the sons of Benjamin were Belah, and Becher, and Ashbel, Gera, and Naaman, Ehi, and Rosh, Muppim, and Huppim, and Ard.

Genesis 49:27
Benjamin shall ravin as a wolf: in the morning he shall devour the prey, and at night he shall divide the spoil.

The descendants of Benjamin sadly did not continue on in the path of obedience.

Judges 20:13 NKJV
Now therefore, deliver up the men, the perverted men who *are* in Gibeah, that we may put them to death and remove the evil from Israel!" But the children of Benjamin would not listen to the voice of their brethren, the children of Israel.

Judges 20:16 NKJV
Among all this people *were* seven hundred select men *who were* left-handed; every one could sling a stone at a hair's *breadth* and not miss.

Judges 20:34 NKJV
And ten thousand select men from all Israel came against Gibeah, and the battle was fierce. But *the Benjamites*[a] did not know that disaster *was* upon them.

Judges 21:3 NJKV
and said, "O LORD God of Israel, why has this come to pass in Israel, that today there should be one tribe *missing* in Israel?"

Judges 21:6 NKJV
And the children of Israel grieved for Benjamin their brother, and said, "One tribe is cut off from Israel today.

Judges 21:13 NKJV
Then the whole congregation sent *word* to the children of Benjamin who *were* at the rock of Rimmon, and announced peace to them.

Judges 21:15 NKJV
And the people grieved for Benjamin, because the LORD had made a void in the tribes of Israel.

Judges 21:17 NKJV
And they said, "*There must be* an inheritance for the survivors of Benjamin, that a tribe may not be destroyed from Israel.

Judges 21:23 NKJV
And the children of Benjamin did so; they took enough wives for their number from those who danced, whom they caught. Then they went and returned to their inheritance, and they rebuilt the cities and dwelt in them.

Benjamin's linage sinned and instead of repenting and receiving punishment they choose to go to war and received judgment instead. Many of their brethren were lost in a war that should have never been. The Benjamites were warriors and they trusted in their ability, but God had already given the word they would be defeated. They fought against their brethren and many of the tribe of Israel were lost as a result. Still their brethren were concerned about what would become of one of them and did not want to see an entire tribe destroyed. God honored them and a small amount of the tribe was saved and given wives so that they could remain in the earth and their heritage could continue.

The Benjamites knew who they were, mighty warriors, but they were anointed to fight by God. God helped them, equipped them, and when you allow disobedience to separate you from God you become powerless and your life falls apart.

Sadly, their lives did become sorrowful, just like the name Benoi meant, but it was by choice, not destiny.

Jacob to Israel

Jacob means heel holder, supplanter

Israel means God prevails, godlike

Jacob is the grandson of the beloved and promised child Isaac.

Genesis 35:10-13

[10] And God said unto him, Thy name is Jacob: thy name shall not be called any more Jacob, but Israel shall be thy name: and he called his name Israel.

[11] And God said unto him, I am God Almighty: be fruitful and multiply; a nation and a company of nations shall be of thee, and kings shall come out of thy loins;

[12] And the land which I gave Abraham and Isaac, to thee I will give it, and to thy seed after thee will I give the land.

[13] And God went up from him in the place where he talked with him.

Notice Jacob's name changed right before the birth of his final son. Just before his favorite wife died and his encounter with the brother he had been estranged from for years. Many times we have to face who we are, our nature, and our motives before we can enter into the promise of God. Jacob's entire life had been that of a trickster and he could not go any further until he faced his nature.

The birthright
Genesis 25:31-34

And Jacob said, Sell me this day thy birthright.
And Esau said, Behold, I am at the point to die: and what profit shall this birthright do to me?
And Jacob said, Swear to me this day; and he sware unto him: and he sold his birthright unto Jacob.
Then Jacob gave Esau bread and pottage of lentiles; and he did eat and drink, and rose up, and went his way: thus Esau despised his birthright.
Now there was no reason in the world that Jacob should not have been willing to feed his own flesh and blood, his twin brother, his family; but instead his resorted to his nature, trickery.

The blessing
Genesis 27:18-43

[18] And he came unto his father, and said, My father: and he said, Here am I; who art thou, my son?

[19] And Jacob said unto his father, I am Esau thy first born; I have done according as thou badest me: arise, I pray thee, sit and eat of my venison, that thy soul may bless me.

[20] And Isaac said unto his son, How is it that thou hast found it so quickly, my son? And he said, Because the LORD thy God brought it to me.

²¹ And Isaac said unto Jacob, Come near, I pray thee, that I may feel thee, my son, whether thou be my very son Esau or not.

²² And Jacob went near unto Isaac his father; and he felt him, and said, The voice is Jacob's voice, but the hands are the hands of Esau.

²³ And he discerned him not, because his hands were hairy, as his brother Esau's hands: so he blessed him.

²⁴ And he said, Art thou my very son Esau? And he said, I am.

²⁵ And he said, Bring it near to me, and I will eat of my son's venison, that my soul may bless thee. And he brought it near to him, and he did eat: and he brought him wine and he drank.

²⁶ And his father Isaac said unto him, Come near now, and kiss me, my son.

²⁷ And he came near, and kissed him: and he smelled the smell of his raiment, and blessed him, and said, See, the smell of my son is as the smell of a field which the LORD hath blessed:

²⁸ Therefore God give thee of the dew of heaven, and the fatness of the earth, and plenty of corn and wine:

²⁹ Let people serve thee, and nations bow down to thee: be lord over thy brethren, and let thy mother's sons bow down to thee: cursed be every one that curseth thee, and blessed be he that blesseth thee.

³⁰ And it came to pass, as soon as Isaac had made an end of blessing Jacob, and Jacob was yet scarce gone out from the presence of Isaac his father, that Esau his brother came in from his hunting.

³¹ And he also had made savoury meat, and brought it unto his father, and said unto his father, Let my father arise, and eat of his son's venison, that thy soul may bless me.

32 And Isaac his father said unto him, Who art thou? And he said, I am thy son, thy firstborn Esau.

33 And Isaac trembled very exceedingly, and said, Who? where is he that hath taken venison, and brought it me, and I have eaten of all before thou camest, and have blessed him? yea, and he shall be blessed.

34 And when Esau heard the words of his father, he cried with a great and exceeding bitter cry, and said unto his father, Bless me, even me also, O my father.

35 And he said, Thy brother came with subtilty, and hath taken away thy blessing.

36 And he said, Is not he rightly named Jacob? for he hath supplanted me these two times: he took away my birthright; and, behold, now he hath taken away my blessing. And he said, Hast thou not reserved a blessing for me?

37 And Isaac answered and said unto Esau, Behold, I have made him thy lord, and all his brethren have I given to him for servants; and with corn and wine have I sustained him: and what shall I do now unto thee, my son?

38 And Esau said unto his father, Hast thou but one blessing, my father? bless me, even me also, O my father. And Esau lifted up his voice, and wept.

39 And Isaac his father answered and said unto him, Behold, thy dwelling shall be the fatness of the earth, and of the dew of heaven from above;

40 And by thy sword shalt thou live, and shalt serve thy brother; and it shall come to pass when thou shalt have the dominion, that thou shalt break his yoke from off thy neck.

41 And Esau hated Jacob because of the blessing wherewith his father

blessed him: and Esau said in his heart, The days of mourning for my father are at hand; then will I slay my brother Jacob.

⁴² And these words of Esau her elder son were told to Rebekah: and she sent and called Jacob her younger son, and said unto him, Behold, thy brother Esau, as touching thee, doth comfort himself, purposing to kill thee.

⁴³ Now therefore, my son, obey my voice; arise, flee thou to Laban my brother to Haran;

Notice what Esau says about his brother in this passage of scripture in Genesis 27:36
And he said, Is not he rightly named Jacob? for he hath supplanted me these two times: he took away my birthright; and, behold, now he hath taken away my blessing. And he said, Hast thou not reserved a blessing for me?

He became godlike and entered into the promise of God when he changed and embraced what God had for him all along.

Genesis 46:2-3
²And God spake unto Israel in the visions of the night, and said, Jacob, Jacob. And he said, Here am I.

³And he said, I am God, the God of thy father: fear not to go down into Egypt; for I will there make of thee a great nation:

Although the Bible continues to refer to him as Israel, God called him Jacob Jacob in his dreams.

His nature had been changed already

Genesis 46:5
⁵And Jacob rose up from Beersheba: and the sons of Israel carried Jacob

their father, and their little ones, and their wives, in the wagons which Pharaoh had sent to carry him.

The Sons of Israel…

Genesis 46:30
³⁰And Israel said unto Joseph, Now let me die, since I have seen thy face, because thou art yet alive.

Genesis 47:6, 9-12
⁶The land of Egypt is before thee; in the best of the land make thy father and brethren to dwell; in the land of Goshen let them dwell: and if thou knowest any men of activity among them, then make them rulers over my cattle.

⁹And Jacob said unto Pharaoh, The days of the years of my pilgrimage are an hundred and thirty years: few and evil have the days of the years of my life been, and have not attained unto the days of the years of the life of my fathers in the days of their pilgrimage.

¹⁰And Jacob blessed Pharaoh, and went out from before Pharaoh.

¹¹And Joseph placed his father and his brethren, and gave them a possession in the land of Egypt, in the best of the land, in the land of Rameses, as Pharaoh had commanded.

¹²And Joseph nourished his father, and his brethren, and all his father's household, with bread, according to their families.

Genesis 47:
²⁷And Israel dwelt in the land of Egypt, in the country of Goshen; and they had possessions therein, and grew, and multiplied exceedingly.

²⁸And Jacob lived in the land of Egypt seventeen years: so the whole age of Jacob was an hundred forty and seven years.

His legacy continued and he served the purpose of God for his life according to the promises of God. Note these power scriptures in Deuteronomy 32:9-14

For the LORD'S portion is his people; Jacob is the lot of his inheritance.

He found him in a desert land, and in the waste howling wilderness; he led him about, he instructed him, he kept him as the apple of his eye.

As an eagle stirreth up her nest, fluttereth over her young, spreadeth abroad her wings, taketh them, beareth them on her wings:

So the LORD alone did lead him, and there was no strange god with him.

He made him ride on the high places of the earth, that he might eat the increase of the fields; and he made him to suck honey out of the rock, and oil out of the flinty rock;

Butter of kine, and milk of sheep, with fat of lambs, and rams of the breed of Bashan, and goats, with the fat of kidneys of wheat; and thou didst drink the pure blood of the grape.

Zacharias to John

Luke 1:57-65
Zacharias means The east wind or storm from the east wind

John means Jehovah has graced

Luke 1:13
But the angel said unto him, Fear not, Zacharias: for thy prayer is heard; and thy wife Elisabeth shall bear thee a son, and thou shalt call his name John.

In this case the family of Zacharias had plans due to his condition and stepped up thinking they were doing him a favor in naming his child. Zacharias, the priest, at this time was unable to speak because of his unbelief when he was told of the promised child. God had sent Gabriel himself that stood before the presence of the Lord to deliver this message and relatives got involved with something that did not concern them. His family members argued that they did not have anybody named John in the family when Elisabeth attempted to carry out the will of her husband. The Bible says "they" called him Zacharias in verse 59 of Luke. Even though his wife spoke up and said, "Not so" "they" didn't take her word for it and got the mute Zacharias involved. You must watch the influence of others in your life, "they" don't know what God has spoken to your heart so that makes what "they" say irrelevant.

It was only when the priest Zacharias got into agreement with the plan of God and wrote down the name John in response to what he should be called did his mouth open and he was able to speak again. What are you holding up because you won't say what God says, believe what He has told you, or haven't written your vision down? Agree with God.

God himself stepped in and gave Solomon a new name.

After the death of David's child born as a result of his affair with Bathsheba God blessed them to conceive again and they called the child Solomon.

2 Samuel 12:24
And David comforted Bathsheba his wife, and went in unto her, and lay with her: and she bare a son, and he called his name Solomon: and the LORD loved him.

2 Samuel 12:25
And he sent by the hand of Nathan the prophet; and he called his name Jedidiah, because of the LORD.

The Lord loved him so he called him by a different name. God Himself gave Solomon a pet name. What compassion and love exemplified in these passages of scriptures. The Lord loved him before his parents ever knew him. Like Solomon, he has called us by name and knew us before we were ever in our mother's womb. He loves us.

Solomon means peace or to be in a covenant of peace

Jedidiah means beloved of the Lord

What does God call you?

Children but Heirs (us)

What does He say about you?

Fearfully and wonderfully made
Made in His image
He will withhold no good thing from you

The world will call you something but God calls you something else. God knows who you really are and what He has planned for you. Don't settle, follow His plans, and answer His call.

It is impossible that God forget us although sometimes our circumstance, our emotions, and even our eyes scream otherwise. The most important thing to remember in times when you feel forgotten, or left behind, or even alone is to REMEMBER. You remember God and everything He has said to you, about you, and promised for you and keep walking in faith. Fall in love with Him and stay in love with Him and it will be the fuel to your faith.

PART 4

My Heart's Cry

Inspirations and Meditations for the Journey

Wait

Wait on him
Concentrate
Don't move
Wait on him
It doesn't matter what anyone else is doing
It doesn't matter what anyone else is thinking
It doesn't matter what anyone else is saying
When their words meet with His they fall to the ground
Don't be anxious
So what it seems you've fallen behind
So what
God is behind you
And in front
And on the sides
And underneath
And on top
And inside
So listen to Him
Wait until you hear

Psalms 139:5
You hem me in—behind and before; you have laid your hand upon me.

Rest

For now I'll just rest
Not stop
Not quit
Rest
Rest in Him and my promise
Rest on Him and His Word
Rest because of Him and my destiny

I'll be at ease in my mind, spirit, and body
Because I know of His commitment toward me

I know about His record
The accuracy of it
How my days are written and numbered
My hairs he's counted himself
He's walked out my steps before He ordered them
To make sure I could follow
In the palms of His hands I have been engraved
Forever before Him

So now
I'll just rest

Staying on track

When I know he sent me
I know he will
Clothe me
Keep me
Befriend me
And when it's time
He will send for me
I will not trouble my mind with the details

I'll remain
Joyful
Peaceful
Content
Motivated

I'll remain
Where he placed me
So he'll be sure to find me when He comes looking for me

I'll remain
So I'll be ready, equipped, have what it takes
To move on to the next dimension
When I'm summoned

I'll remain
So I can remain

Be real

I say God I'm scared
I'll protect you He says

I say God I don't know how
He says I'll teach you now

I say Lord I can't see
He says follow me

I say Lord I want to
He says I know it's true

I say Lord I need you here
He says I am always near

Fit for duty

You cannot carry the weights of offense
In the line of duty they make your heart sick

You cannot carry the restraints of pride
In the heart of the battle
Your arms will be tied

You cannot wear the muzzle of doubt
Or surely your war cry will never get out

You cannot wear the chains of fear
In the wrong direction they can only steer

Disciple determined destined

Disciple enough not to be detoured by distractions
Determined enough not to be detained by the devour
Destined enough not to demean or demur His deity in delay
Determined enough to disallow debility and depression to demolish my
dreams
Destined enough to know that dilemmas and deferments do not divert
the Divine

When I know my captivity was orchestrated by God

My realizing it was God that brought me to my present state is vital. Otherwise I will exhaust myself finding fault with and being angry at people, and trying to get out of all the wrong things.

I should not ask why? But my question should be what?

What next God?

Refuse to conform to the conditions

I will not become a product of where I've been
I will dictate to my circumstances they will not dictate to me
I will not be a statistic
I am unique
I can come through unusual circumstances without wearing the residue
of my experiences
I will not conform
I'm passing through
I will not habitat

I must challenge them

Sickness you can't hold me against my will
Death you can't have me
Pain you can't hold me
Poverty you can't have me
You don't own me
Sin you can't keep me
Disobedience I release myself from you

Serenity

Settle down, listen
You're o.k.
Though it seems to be barren
It won't remain that way

Out of death always comes life
In a little while you'll be alright
Settle down
It's not your fight

Settle down peace be unto you
This is a battle you can't lose
It's really o.k.
In a barren land there is still a way

It's really not a big deal
All the rivers He will refill
He'll cause the trees to produce fruit
And everything will come up by the root

Settle down
Don't let it be deadness that you see
See the life underneath

I see you even in the darkness

Darkness cannot hide Him
He is light
I see His hand beckoning me to keep going
I see His feet lighting up the path for me to follow
I see His face
The glorious Father
He consumes the dark so I can focus only on Him
I only had to shift my vision
Put on my 3D glasses
Determined
Disciplined
Destined
So I could see Him
Not the darkness

Get to the root

I've been a prisoner of many things
But when I decided to take a look at all those things
I figured they were all linked to one thing
Fear

It cause me to become sick
It caused me to withdraw
It caused me to stop
So it had to be stopped from its influence in my life

Elijah had to face this to stop running from Jezebel
Moses had to face this even after taking Aaron with him
Timothy had to face this after Paul's imprisonment
I was no different

Fear of failure
Fear of success
Fear of missing the mark
Fear of being different

I had to turn around
Stand flat-footed and face it
Shaking in my boots
But I refused to run anymore

Deliverance

The same thing that brought me here
Will be the same thing that delivers me
It is because of my destiny that I came
And it will be because of my destiny that I will leave
It will deliver me
Otherwise my purpose will not be complete
I can rest assured
This is not the end

I shall overcome

I can live in poverty but it cannot live in me
For sooner or later poverty must set me free

I can live in the slums but it will never be what I'll become
Soon my feet will take wings and from here I'll run

I can live in debt
My mind is at peace I'll still rest
Because without a doubt I'll know success

Yeah I've been sick
My body he did afflict
But as the sunrise in the morning my health He did fix

I did know shame and all of its pain
But the God in me it could not contain
I was brought forth in glory without a stain

Dare I be happy?

Dare I be happy?
Full of joy
Dare I explore my future?
All open doors
Dare I look around?
In my surrounding and find joy
In the eyes of a girl or a baby boy
Dare I look and see peace
In the birds in the trees
Dare I bubble over with a laugh?
At the sound of a joke only told half
YES!

The Link

You were the link to the dynasty
It was never about you
You were the
Rehab
Joshua
David
Zerrubabel
If you did not make it
Many others would not have made it
I sent you ahead
To prepare the way
To make it easy for those coming behind you
I chose you because I knew you could

Deliverance

The same thing that brought me here
Will be the same thing that delivers me
It is because of my destiny that I came
And it will be because of my destiny that I will leave
It will deliver me
Otherwise my destiny will not be complete
I can rest assured
This is not the end

Washing Word

Waters to make you clean
Flowing from the rivers stream
The greatness of its cleansing power
Relieving, soothing from the mire—
By the river's bed
To rest your head
Peace of mind no dread
Resting in its glow
To be troubled no more

Say a prayer

Say a prayer
Dare believe
Till you receive

Say a prayer
Dare wait
Till prayer equals fate

Who

I don't understand why
But I must understand who
Who is in control
Who knows and sees all
Who has the power
Who is with me
Who created me
Who keeps me
Who will deliver me

Daily

Every day I feel your hand gently waking me, strengthening me
Leading me
Supporting me
Every day I take your hand you
Guide me
Feed me
Cover me
Every day I make the decision to walk
In the direction of your choice there is provision

The mind

It's clear
It's focused
It's settled
Unmovable
Thoughts are pure
Of love
Of hope
Of growth
Determined

Fight

Fight
For yourself
For who you are and why you came
To get up and not in the present state remain
Fight
To keep your sanity
Don't let it be a prison you see
Fight
To prosper in the place where you are
To keep the doors of hope ajar
Fight
As if you have everything to lose
And become a vessel God can use

Questions

Why must I hurt this way?
Why does it have to be so difficult?
Why do I feel like I'm being torn apart?
Why can't I seem to get out?
Was it ordained?
How is it that I have no name?
Can this be your hand pruning me?
Cutting away all the dead things
Could it be you're causing me to grow?
So I can bear fruit
Be productive again
Could it be?
And if so
Why didn't I know?

The trick

You were after my praise
That's why that stupid offence came
I couldn't even see it
Your dirty little trick
But I was the wrong one that you picked
I've learned to praise Him even when things are bad
I found it was the only treasure I had
Tucked away deep inside my heart
One for every occasion
From finish to start
Even in tears I still have a praise
So it looks like you lost at your little charade

So

So what
He's still amazing
He still makes my heart go crazy
He is still my man
And we'll be together forever
Just like He planned
He's still my hero
The man I married so long ago
The one that has the ability to make me smile
The one that told me I'm His child

Focus

I see darkness all around me
So I must rely on touch about my world
But touch it surely hurt
Is this what it is like as black as the night

I see shadows and shapes
Lines and circles in the heat of the day
In the distance spheres and rays
Is this what's associated with my pain

I see a glimpse of light
Just enough to challenge the night
Little sparks here and there
Leading me to whom to where

I see the sun as bright as day
And the cloud and the trees saying this way
I see the Father's face
It came into focus by my praise

Psalms 139:12
Even the darkness will not be dark to you, the night will shine like the
day, for darkness is as light to you.

Pressure

The very thing I thought would destroy me
Is pushing me into my destiny
It is causing me to lunge unto my prophetic promise
It's working for me
The very thing that was sent to destroy me
Is under my control
The roles have been reversed
The pressure is building me upward
The pain is giving me the power
To continue
To endure
To finish
He knew it would

PART 5

A Meditation of Restoration

The following meditation is a Psalm that many people know and use for various reasons throughout life. It is one of my favorite and I like to refer to it as, "a meditation of restoration." When things become challenging in life, and this is guaranteed, I find solace just thinking about these written words. I encourage you to take some time and read these words, pausing with each new sentence and see what a difference it will make in your life.

A Meditation of Restoration
Ps 23 NKJV
(Emphasis the author's)

Psalms 23

The Lord is...
My Maker
All Powerful
My Defense
My Savior
All Knowing
My Strong tower
My Healer
Everywhere at all times
My Help
My Peace
My Comforter
I am never alone

The Lord is my shepherd;...
He Guides Me
He Leads Me
He Protects Me
He Feeds Me
He Surrounds Me

The Lord is my shepherd; I shall not want...
For any good thing
Not Emotionally
Not Physically
Not Spiritually
I lack nothing

The Lord is my shepherd; I shall not want. He makes me...
Whole
Nothing missing nothing broken
Perfect and entire
In His Image
In His Likeness

Righteous
Well

The Lord is my shepherd; I shall not want. He makes me to lie down in green pastures;…
Where there is Life
Strength
Restoration
Hope
Healing
More than Enough

The Lord is my shepherd; I shall not want. He makes me to lie down in green pastures; He leads me beside the still waters…
Where He visits me each day
Where He instructs me
Where He tells me His will
In His peace
In His presence
In His protection
In His prosperity
Where I rest

The Lord is my shepherd; I shall not want. He makes me to lie down in green pastures; He leads me besides the still waters. He restores my soul;…
Breathes life back into me again
Reaffirms His love for me
Reminds me of who I am
Consoles me
Comforts me
Adorns me with His love
Shows me His salvation

The Lord is my shepherd; I shall not want. He makes me to lie down in green pastures; He leads me beside the still waters. He

restores my soul; He leads me...
To places I've never dreamed
In the steps He has orchestrated
From pain to peace
From darkness to light
From sorrow to joy and dancing
To wells of living water
Into perfect worship
By His Spirit

The Lord is my shepherd; I shall not want. He makes me to lie down in green pastures; He leads me beside the still waters. He restores my soul; He leads me in the paths of righteousness...
Paved with the blood of Jesus
Marked with wisdom
Laden with understanding
Governed by His knowledge
Sealed with His love
Covered by mercy

The Lord is my shepherd; I shall not want. He makes me to lie down in green pastures; He leads me beside the still waters. He restores my soul; He leads me in the paths of righteousness For His name's sake...
He will bless me
He will never leave me
He will hear me when I cry
He will rescue me
He will honor me
He will keep me
I will succeed

The Lord is my shepherd; I shall not want. He makes me to lie down in green pastures; He leads me beside the still waters. He restores my soul; He leads me in the paths of righteousness for His name's sake. Yea ...
I will have trouble but I will come through it

I will follow hard after Him
I will seek His face
I will love Him
Honor Him
Respect Him
Trust Him
Not leave Him

The Lord is my shepherd; I shall not want. He makes me to lie down in green pastures; He leads me beside the still waters. He restores my soul; He leads me in the paths of righteousness for His name's sake. Yea though I walk...
He will walk with me
My angels will accompany me
His Word will speak to me
I am not alone
His Spirit will guide me
My steps are ordered
I have a plain path
I will not turn to the left or to the right

The Lord is my shepherd; I shall not want. He makes me to lie down in green pastures; He leads me beside the still waters. He restores my soul; He leads me in the paths of righteousness for His name's sake. Yea though I walk through the valley of the shadow...
I have shelter
He intercedes for me
His glory is my rear guard
His arm is not too short to save me
I have His attention
I have His promises
He made the valley
Nothing shall by any means harm me
I am secure
There is no shadow of turning in Him

The Lord is my shepherd; I shall not want. He makes me to lie

down in green pastures; He leads me beside the still waters. He restores my soul; He leads me in the paths of righteousness for His name's sake. Yea though I walk through the valley of the shadow of death,...

Can't stop me [He defeated it]
He satisfies me with long life
I live healthy long and strong
I am crucified with Him, yet I live
I live by the power of God within me
The same Spirit that raised Christ from the dead is in me
I do all things through Christ who strengthens me
I have the grace of God

The Lord is my shepherd; I shall not want. He makes me to lie down in green pastures; He leads me beside the still waters. He restores my soul; He leads me in the paths of righteousness for His name's sake. Yea though I walk through the valley of the shadow of death, I will fear no evil;...

It will not befall me
No calamity
No destruction
Will come upon me
I will not be seized with alarm
I am quiet from the fear of evil
You deliver me from evil
You keep me from the violent man
Goodness and mercy are my escorts
He has given me personal angels for the journey

The Lord is my shepherd; I shall not want. He makes me to lie down in green pastures; He leads me beside the still waters. He restores my soul; He leads me in the paths of righteousness for His name's sake. Yea though I walk through the valley of the shadow of death, I will fear no evil; For you...

Who made the heavens and the earth
Attend to me personally
Are a strong tower

Do not sleep
Are my defense
Are God
The great I AM
Faithful
Can not lie
Bless me when I come
Bless me when I go
Will get the glory out of my life

The Lord is my shepherd; I shall not want. He makes me to lie down in green pastures; He leads me beside the still waters. He restores my soul; He leads me in the paths of righteousness for His name's sake. Yea though I walk through the valley of the shadow of death, I will fear no evil; For you art with me;...
I am not alone
Your Spirit is with me
Goodness and Mercy are here
My angels are here
The Word living breathing Jesus is here
The Blood is covering me
All is well

The Lord is my shepherd; I shall not want. He makes me to lie down in green pastures; He leads me beside the still waters. He restores my soul; He leads me in the paths of righteousness for His name's sake. Yea though I walk through the valley of the shadow of death, I will fear no evil; for you art with me; Your rod and your staff, they comfort me. You prepare a table before me...
Specifically with what I need and want
Created with me in mind
We eat together (you and I)
I forget my surroundings
I feast on your Word
You have given all things to enjoy

The Lord is my shepherd; I shall not want. He makes me to lie

down in green pastures; He leads me beside the still waters. He restores my soul; He leads me in the paths of righteousness for His name's sake. Yea though I walk through the valley of the shadow of death, I will fear no evil; For you art with me; Your rod and your staff, they comfort me You prepare a table before me in the presence of my enemies;...

I succeed

I come out of trouble

I prosper

I am protected

I have more than enough

I am surrounded by your favor

The Lord is my shepherd; I shall not want. He makes me to lie down in green pastures; He leads me beside the still waters. He restores my soul; He leads me in the paths of righteousness for His name's sake. Yea though I walk through the valley of the shadow of death, I will fear no evil; For you art with me; Your rod and your staff, they comfort me. You prepare a table before me in the presence of my enemies; you anoint my head with oil;

I have a fresh anointing

You cleanse me

Prepare me for your purpose

Love me as only you can

Set me aside for your purpose

I am full of the Holy Ghost

The Lord is my shepherd; I shall not want. He makes me to lie down in green pastures; He leads me beside the still waters. He restores my soul; He leads me in the paths of righteousness for His name's sake. Yea though I walk through the valley of the shadow of death, I will fear no evil; For you art with me; Your rod and your staff, they comfort me You prepare a table before me in the presence of my enemies; you anoint my head with oil My cup runs over...

Filled with blessings daily

Filled with healing

Filled with love
Filled with joy and peace
Have everything I need to the over flowing

The Lord is my shepherd; I shall not want. He makes me to lie down in green pastures; He leads me beside the still waters. He restores my soul; He leads me in the paths of righteousness for His name's sake. Yea though I walk through the valley of the shadow of death, I will fear no evil; For you art with me; Your rod and your staff, they comfort me You prepare a table before me in the presence of my enemies; you anoint my head with oil My cup runs over surely goodness and mercy shall follow me…
My body guards
Your glory
Your mighty out stretched hand
Your power to save
Your power to heal
Your power to deliver
Your power to sustain

The Lord is my shepherd; I shall not want. He makes me to lie down in green pastures; beside the still waters. He restores my soul; He leads me in the paths of righteousness for His name's sake. Yea though I walk through the valley of the shadow of death, I will fear no evil; For you art with me; Your rod and your staff, they comfort me You prepare a table before me in the presence of my enemies; You anoint my head with oil; My cup runs over. Surely goodness and mercy shall follow me All the days of my life;…
I will dwell safe and be quiet from the fear of evil
I will walk upright before Him
I will trust you
I will follow hard after you

The Lord is my shepherd; I shall not want. He makes me to lie down in green pastures; He leads me beside the still waters. He restores my soul; He leads me in the paths of righteousness For His name's sake. Yea, though I walk through the valley of the shadow

of death, I will fear no evil; For you art with me; Your rod and your staff, they comfort me You prepare a table before me in the presence of my enemies; You anoint my head with oil; My cup runs over. Surely goodness and mercy shall follow me All the days of my life and I will...

Honor Him

Be secure in Him

Love Him

Respect Him

Obey Him

Hear Him say well done

The Lord is my shepherd; I shall not want. He makes me to lie down in green pastures; He leads me beside the still waters. He restores my soul; He leads me in the paths of righteousness for His name's sake. Yea though I walk through the valley of the shadow of death, I will fear no evil; For you art with me; Your rod and your staff, they comfort me You prepare a table before me in the presence of my enemies; you anoint my head with oil My cup runs over surely goodness and mercy shall follow me all the days of my life and I will dwell in the house of the Lord Forever...

My life has been settled

I will see your face in peace

My days are written in your book

And with each new day I will know you more and more

Amen (So Be It)